A catalogue record for this book is available from the British Library

Published by Ladybird Books Ltd
27 Wrights Lane  London  W8 5TZ
A Penguin Company

2 4 6 8 10 9 7 5 3 1

LADYBIRD and the device of a Ladybird are trademarks of Ladybird Books Ltd

# Disney's DINOSAUR

Long ago a herd of dinosaurs lived happily in the Nesting Grounds. Every day the tall, long-necked dinosaurs took it in turns to look out for their enemies, the Carnotaurs. They knew that these dangerous meat-eating dinosaurs were always hiding in the forests nearby.

Early one morning, a fierce Carnotaur charged out of the trees and attacked the herd.

A mother dinosaur bravely defended her nest. But as the Carnotaur ran past her, a hungry lizard stole one of the eggs from the nest.

The lizard ran off into the forest and dropped the egg into a stream. The egg was carried along towards a wide river, where a bird picked it up.

The bird flew across the ocean and at last, after many miles, dropped the egg down onto Lemur Island – where it hatched right in front of a family of lemurs!

Plio, a young female lemur, gently picked up the newly-hatched baby dinosaur.

"It's a meat-eating monster from across the sea!" cried her father, Yar.

"Looks like a baby to me," Plio answered softly. "Anyway, we'll teach him to hate meat."

Zini, their lemur friend, agreed with Plio.

So the young dinosaur grew up among the friendly lemurs on Lemur Island.

The lemurs named the dinosaur Aladar. They watched as the tiny baby grew into a giant Iguanodon. But big as he was, Aladar still acted gently and kindly towards the lemurs. He even treated Plio's daughter, Suri, like a little sister!

One terrible day, Yar sniffed the air.

"Something's wrong!" he said suddenly.

Plio sensed the danger, too. "Aladar! Find Suri!" she cried.

Across the sea, a huge comet had fallen to earth. And an enormous fireball was pushing through the water towards Lemur Island!

Aladar ran quickly to pick up Plio and Suri, while Yar and Zini jumped onto his back.

Aladar raced across Lemur Island, until he came to the edge of a cliff. He looked back and saw the fireball close behind them. There was no choice – he had to jump into the sea far below.

Aladar swam with his friends across the sea to the mainland.

When they reached the shore, they looked back sadly at Lemur Island. They knew that their home had been destroyed.

But they still had one another, and the next day they would set out to look for a new home.

As the sun rose, a big herd of dinosaurs stomped past them. Two kind old dinosaurs followed slowly at the back of the herd. Their names were Baylene and Eema.

Aladar was amazed to see so many creatures like him. So he and the lemurs decided to join the old dinosaurs on their journey. Soon they became friends.

Baylene and Eema explained that the dinosaurs were on their way to the Nesting Grounds.

The herd travelled quickly. There was no food or water because the fireball had dried up most of the land.

Aladar became worried about Baylene and Eema. They could not keep up with the rest of the herd.

"Maybe you could slow down a bit?" Aladar suggested to Kron, the dinosaur leader.

But Kron didn't care about the weaker ones and he didn't like Aladar – he thought that Aladar wanted to take his place as leader.

The next morning, the herd set off early. The dinosaurs all needed water and they knew that it would take nearly a whole day to walk to the nearest lake.

As Aladar waited for the lemurs to climb up onto his neck, he noticed Kron's sister Neera. She had been watching him.

Aladar stood very still. He watched her as she moved off with the herd. Aladar liked her – a lot!

As they approached the lake, Bruton, one of Kron's look-outs, hurried towards them. He had seen some Carnotaurs and they were close behind.

"We can't stop long at the lake," warned Bruton. "The Carnotaurs will catch up and attack us."

But, when they did reach the lake, there was even more bad news. The water had been dried up by the fireball.

The rest of the herd moved sadly forward.

As Aladar helped his two old friends through the deep sand, he noticed that Baylene's footprints had filled with water. "Look!" he shouted, and all the friends gathered round to dig.

Everyone heard, and all the dinosaurs charged back towards the new water hole. Aladar tried his best to protect his friends from the stampede.

Then, when everything was quiet at last, he helped two small orphaned dinosaurs to get a drink. Neera came up to them.

"Why did you help the old ones?" Neera asked him.

"If we watch out for each other, we will all stand a chance of surviving," said Aladar.

Neera was amazed. She'd never met a dinosaur before who cared as much for others as Aladar did.

At the same moment, Bruton stumbled over to Kron. Bruton had been away from the herd, watching out for their enemies. Now he was badly wounded.

"Carnotaurs!" he exclaimed weakly. "Go quickly! Leave me behind!"

So Kron ordered the herd to move out at double speed.

Aladar and Neera rushed towards Kron. "The others at the back," cried Aladar, "they'll never make it! They need to rest."

But Kron wouldn't listen. He lunged at Aladar, ready for a fight.

"Aladar, just go!" begged Neera. She didn't want him to get hurt.

Aladar and his friends watched sadly as the herd moved away. They were on their own now, and the sky above them darkened with a storm.

Not far away they heard a painful cry.

"It's Bruton!" exclaimed Eema. And they helped him into a cave to shelter.

Bruton was surprised by their kindness. But before he could thank them, some Carnotaurs entered the cave and attacked!

"I'll hold them off!" Bruton yelled bravely to Aladar. "Save yourself!" So Aladar led the others to safety deep inside the cave.

Bruton chased the Carnotaurs out into the stormy night, but he was injured. And, though Aladar went back to help him, it was too late.

Meanwhile Kron pushed the herd onwards. Neera walked slowly with the two orphaned dinosaurs. At last one of them stopped. He was exhausted.

"It's okay, little ones," Neera said kindly. "We're going to make it," she added, and nudged them along.

At the back of the cave, Zini smelled fresh air. It was a way out! And they all started digging.

At last they crashed through the rocks – but then stopped, amazed. The Nesting Grounds stretched before them, green and beautiful, with a large blue lake in the middle.

But Aladar was worried. There was no sign of the rest of the herd, and a landslide blocked the main entrance to the valley.

Determined to save Neera and the others, Aladar left his friends to rest in the Nesting Grounds. He set out alone to look for the herd.

When Aladar found the dinosaurs at last, Kron was trying to push them up and over the landslide. It was far too dangerous.

"I know a way into the valley, and everybody can make it!" Aladar cried out. "Follow me!"

Neera and the others started to follow, but Kron was furious. Now he was certain that Aladar was trying to take over the leadership of the herd.

Suddenly Kron attacked Aladar and knocked him to the ground. Kron ordered the herd to climb the landslide.

Neera refused and stayed to help Aladar. Together they began to lead the rest of the herd towards the cave. But they turned straight into the path of an enormous Carnotaur.

Aladar stood firm. "Don't move!" he called to the other dinosaurs. "Stand together!" Then Aladar started to bellow, and soon the rest of the herd joined in.

Frightened by the roar of so many dinosaurs, the Carnotaur started to back away. But then the beast saw Kron, alone on the landslide, and he charged towards him. Kron was hurled to the ground, fatally wounded. Then the rocks collapsed under the Carnotaur and he disappeared from sight.

Neera called out to Kron, but she knew it was no good. Safe, but also saddened, Aladar and Neera nuzzled each other.

The rest of the herd roared its thanks. Now they could finish their journey at last.

Several weeks later, Aladar stood beside Neera in the Nesting Grounds. One of their eggs cracked open and a beautiful baby dinosaur crawled out. Their dinosaur and lemur friends all cheered.

As the valley filled with sunshine and many sounds of joy, everyone was happy. Together they had found their new home.